OUR SLEEPYSAURUS

Our flats used to be brilliant.
Then the Mean Man came.

OUR
SLEEPYSAURUS

Written by
MARTIN WADDELL

Illustrated by
CLIVE SCRUTON

WALKER BOOKS
LONDON

For Rose, in whose garden it grew

First published 1988 by
Walker Books Ltd, 87 Vauxhall Walk
London SE11 5HJ

Paperback edition published 1989

Text © 1988 Martin Waddell
Illustrations © 1988 Clive Scruton

First printed 1988
Printed in Great Britain by
Richard Clay Ltd, Bungay, Suffolk

British Library Cataloguing in Publication Data
Waddell, Martin
Our sleepysaurus.
I. Title II. Scruton, Clive
823'.914[J]   PZ7

ISBN 0-7445-0821-5
ISBN 0-7445-0831-2 Pbk

CONTENTS

Rashid is the one with glasses, and Niki has the bubblegum and I'm the one in the floppy hat.

OUR
SLEEPYSAURUS

I'm Marigold and this is Rashid and Niki. Rashid is the one with glasses, and Niki has the bubblegum and I'm the one in the floppy hat. We live in Bell Street Flats with our mums and dads and the Old Ladies.

Our flats used to be brilliant. Then a man came and put up a sign:

BELL STREET FLATS
NO PETS ALLOWED

"No dogs?" I said.

"No dogs," said the man. "They bark all day."

"No cats?" said Niki.

"No cats," said the man. "They screech all night."

"No goldfish?" said Rashid.

"No goldfish," said the man.

"Why not?" said Rashid. "What do goldfish do? They don't bark and they don't screech..."

"No goldfish because *I say so*!" said the man.

He was a real Mean Man. He kept nosing around, pet-hunting.

We hid tadpoles in the water tank, but he found them. We had robins in the roof space, but he bust up the nest and scared them away. He wouldn't even let our mice stay in the cellar.

Then the Sleepysaurus came.

We didn't know it was a Sleepysaurus at first, because none of us had ever seen one. We thought it was a pile of old rocks. It was

He was a real Mean Man. He kept
nosing around, pet-hunting.

Rashid who saw it first.

"Look at that," he said. "The Mean Man has left a pile of rocks over by the Old Ladies' seat."

Then Niki spotted the hole in the fence.

"Who did that, Marigold?" she said to me.

And I said, "Must have been the Mean Man, moving in his rocks."

Then we found the footprints. Each one was as big as a baby's bath, with claw marks round it. We followed the footprints right across our play area, straight *through* the fence and into the Builder's yard next door. The Builder saw us in his yard, and he came out of his hut, looking very cross.

"What have you kids been doing?" he shouted. "Breaking up my yard?"

We all ran away, but later we came back to have another look.

Something had pulped up the Builder's

pipes. Something had munched up the Builder's cement mixer. Something had chewed
the Builder's concrete. And something had
sat down on his soft cement.

"Looks like an elephant has been here!"
said Niki.

"Or a dinosaur!" I said.

"Or a great-big brontosaurus!" said
Rashid.

"It wasn't," said a yawny voice. "It was
me!"

We all jumped.

"Who said that?" said Rashid.

"Dunno!" said Niki.

"A g-g-g-host!" I said.

And we all ran away, because we don't
like ghosts, especially yawny ghosts, with
footprints as big as a baby's bath, and claw
marks.

Next day the Mean Man came. He saw

the hole in the fence, and the footprints, and the pile of rocks. He was very cross.

"You keep your diggers off my flats!" he told the Builder. "And no dumping rocks!"

The Builder was very cross too.

"You stop those kids from mucking about with my materials!" he told the Mean Man. And he showed the Mean Man the pulped pipes and the munched mixer and chewed concrete and the cement-something-had-sat-on.

"Kids couldn't do that!" said the Mean Man.

"Who did then?" said the Builder.

They got very cross. They started to shout at each other, and then they started to throw things.

It was very funny.

"Who do you think did it?" said Niki.

"Don't know," said Rashid.

"Haven't a clue!" I said. But I wasn't telling the truth. I had a Big Clue. I had more than one Big Clue. I had lots. Lots of footprints as big as a baby's bath, and a yawny voice, and a pile of rocks. I knew what I was going to do.

That night everything was quiet. Mum was in bed and Dad was in bed, Rashid and Niki were in bed, but I don't know about the Old Ladies.

I crept out on to our balcony and prepared for Marigold's Midnight Ghost Watch, for a ghost with big feet and a yawny voice.

Down in the yard, something stirred. There was a creaky, scrapy sound, and the pile of rocks M-O-V-E-D.

Scraaaaaaaak this way and *craaaaaaaaaak* that way. *Scraaaak, craaaaak, scraaaaaaak, craaaaaaak*...the rock pile lurched right across our play area, to the coal bunker.

Then MUNCH!

MUNCH!

MUNCH!

SLURP!

GURGLE!

it swallowed the lot!

"Yummy!" said the rock pile. It licked its lips and headed for the boiler.

"Don't eat that!" I shouted.

"Why not?" said the rock pile, turning its big head slowly to look up at me.

"That's our boiler," I said. "It heats the flats. If you eat it, the Old Ladies will all catch cold for Christmas!"

"What shall I eat then?" it said.

"Wait," I said, and I went to look in our fridge.

"Eggs and bacon and cheese and lettuce and cauliflower and a pork chop," I said.

"That's a big dinner."

"Just a snack for a Sleepysaurus," said the pile of rocks, and it ate the lot, with one big SLURP, followed by a GURGLE as the eggs and bacon and cheese and lettuce and cauliflower and the pork chop all went down inside.

"What...what *is* a Sleepysaurus?" I asked, nervously.

"I am," said the Sleepysaurus.

"But what...what does a Sleepysaurus *do*?" I said.

"I eat, and I sleep," said the Sleepysaurus, settling down comfortably.

"But..."

ZZZZZZZZZZZZZZZZZZZZZZZZZZZ!

The Sleepysaurus didn't talk any more. It had gone to sleep.

Next day I showed the Sleepysaurus to Rashid and Niki.

"Yummy!" said the rock pile.

It licked its lips and headed for the boiler.

"That isn't a Sleepysaurus," said Niki. "That's just a pile of old rocks."

"No, it isn't," I said. "It's got legs and a head and it walks about and eats things."

"Don't believe you!" said Rashid and Niki.

"You wait and see, tonight," I said.

So, that night, we all kept a Sleepysaurus watch on our balconies.

And...

. . . long after everybody had gone to bed . . . the Sleepysaurus moved.

Scraaak this way and *craaak* that way.

Scraaak, craaak, scraaak, craaak. The Sleepysaurus moved across the yard.

MUNCH!

"Hey!" Niki shouted. "Don't eat that! That's my bike!"

"Oh," said the Sleepysaurus. "Sorry."

"And that one's mine," said Rashid. "Put it down."

"*So* sorry," said the Sleepysaurus, blinking its big eyes at us. "I eat a lot," it explained. "Every time I wake up, I have a little walk, and I eat a bit, and then I go back to sleep."

"We'll feed you!" said Niki.

And she went up to her flat and got black olives, feta cheese, half a dozen strawberry yoghurts and five big watermelon slices.

"Very nice," said the Sleepysaurus. "Any more?"

"I'll get some," said Rashid, and he brought last night's curry, samosas, nan bread, onion bhajia and three packets of non-fattening oven chips from his fridge.

"Very nice," said the Sleepysaurus. "Very nice, for a change anyway, but it's not what I'm used to."

"What do you usually eat?" I asked.

"Cement and bricks and coal and concrete and old tin," said the Sleepysaurus.

I looked at Rashid, and Rashid looked at Niki, and we said "G-R-E-A-T!" because we all knew the answer to that.

It was the dump next door, on the other side of the flats from the Builder's Yard.

"We'll get the old pram and wheel you round a dinner every night," we told the Sleepysaurus.

The Sleepysaurus was very pleased, and so were we.

"You can be our pet, and live here for ever," said Rashid.

But the next day the Mean Man came.

The Old Ladies had complained about all the noises the Sleepysaurus was making.

"Are you kids keeping noisy pets in the

The Old Ladies got really mad!
"We're keeping our rock garden!" they shouted.

flats?" the Mean Man shouted at us, in a very mean way. "I told you NO PETS!"

"We haven't had much time for pets," I said. "We've been too busy turning this pile of old rocks into a rock garden for the Old Ladies!"

"How nice!" said the Old Ladies. "A rock garden for us!"

"You can't build a rock garden without making noises," I told the Mean Man.

"I don't know what this place is coming to," said the Mean Man. "Rocks, mess, noises!"

"Never mind about the noises!" said the Old Ladies. "Who cares? We want our garden!"

"Nonsense!" said the Mean Man. "I'm in charge here. I want all this lot cleared away at once!"

The Old Ladies got really mad!

"We're keeping our rock garden!" they shouted, and they all sat down on the Sleepysaurus.

"You move it, and you'll have to move us first!" said the Old Ladies.

They made big signs saying:

OLD
LADIES   and   SAVE
RULE OK!   OUR ROCK
                           GARDEN!

                 WE SHALL   MEAN
and   NOT BE   and   MAN MUST
                 MOVED!   GO!

They waved the signs at the Mean Man and called him names.

The Mean Man got really scared of the Old Ladies. "Oh, all right then!" he grumbled. "Have your rock garden! But don't come complaining to me about noises."

That's how the Sleepysaurus came to our flats.

It lives there all the time.

Each night it goes *scraaak* and *craaak* round the yard. And it munch-slurp-gurgles all the rubbish we can bring it from the dump.

Then it sits down and goes to sleep.

The Old Ladies put seeds on it and watched them grow into big flowers. We've given them ear plugs, so they don't hear the scraaak-craaak-munch-slurp-gurgling noises at night.

They're all happy, and so are we and so is the Sleepysaurus. Our flats are brilliant now!

Everybody says so.

It was very hot. The sun was like a fried egg. Our yard was like a frying pan.

SLEEPYSAURUS
TAKES A BATH

It was very hot. The sun was like a fried egg. Our yard was like a frying pan.

"I'm a melted Marigold," I said.

"And I'm a roasted Rashid!" said Rashid.

"And I'm a nurdled Niki," said Niki. Nurdled isn't a proper word but we all knew what she meant.

My mum went up on the roof in her bikini and Rashid's mum made us cold drinks and Niki's dad put ice cubes down our backs.

The Old Ladies took off their cardigans and sat round the Sleepysaurus, complaining about the heat. The Mean Man came in his dirty vest and told my mum to put on her clothes. My dad told him to clear off. Everybody was hot and cross. Our Sleepysaurus didn't say a thing, but there was steam coming off it.

Then Rashid got the Mean Man's hose. *Woosh!* I got soaked. Niki got drenched. Then we got Rashid. He got sploshed!

"Squirt us!" cried the Old Ladies. We shot the water high in the air, and they all danced about.

"A-a-a-h!" sighed the Sleepysaurus, though nobody heard it but me, because the Old Ladies were making so much noise dancing.

"Stop that at once!" said the Mean Man. I was working the hose pipe and didn't see him coming round the coal shed! SWISH! SWOOSH! SWASH! The Mean Man was washed away. He got up, drippy-puddle coloured, but his vest looked cleaner. Not *much* cleaner, only a bit, because it was a very dirty vest to begin with.

"About time you had a bath!" cried all the Old Ladies. The Mean Man was very cross.

"Who did that?" he shouted. And then he slipped, and fell down *again* in the puddle. His bottom got wet. All the Old Ladies cheered! The Mean Man stepped out of his puddle and chased us. Rashid hid in the bike shed, Niki hid behind the Old Ladies and I hid behind a rock on the Sleepy-saurus. The Mean Man almost got me, but then the Sleepysaurus hissed. I heard it, and the Mean Man heard it, but no one else did. The Mean Man was scared. He went away, but he took his hose with him.

"Thank you very much, Sleepysaurus," I whispered to the Sleepysaurus, but the Sleepysaurus didn't creak or move or do anything, in case it scared the Old Ladies.

We went on being very hot. We all had iced drinks and our mums and dads had iced beer. The Old Ladies started having a tea party on the Sleepysaurus, but the tea was too hot, so my dad gave them iced beer instead.

The Sleepysaurus gave a sort of sigh. I heard it, and Rashid heard it, and Niki heard it too, in spite of all the noise the Old Ladies were making with their beer.

"It's thirsty!" I told Rashid and Niki.

But we didn't know what to do about it. The Sleepysaurus could drink baths and baths and baths of water.

"Wait till tonight!" I told the Sleepy-saurus. "We'll think of something."

The Sleepysaurus lay there in the sun getting hotter and hotter and hotter, and we all thought a lot.

"We can't carry *baths*," said Niki.

"And the Mean Man has taken away the hose pipe," said Rashid.

"What about buckets?" I said.

We got our buckets, and then we looked at the Sleepysaurus.

"How many bucketfuls do we need?" I asked Rashid and Niki.

"Hundreds!" said Rashid.

"Thousands!" said Niki.

"Millions!" I said.

"Billions!" said Rashid.

"Trillions!" said Niki.

"Hundreds of thousands of millions of billions of trillions!" I said. "And there's only one tap in the yard!"

So we gave up the buckets. We thought it might be all right when the sun went down, but it wasn't. Everybody had gone into the flats to complain about sunburn, and everybody was putting oil on everybody else and all the mums and dads and Old Ladies were looking at their red noses and boiled backs. We all came down to the yard.

The Sleepysaurus was *scraaaking* and *craaaking* and *pa-pa-pa-panting* away, just like a big puppy.

"I bet it's very hot," I said.

"I sure am!" panted the Sleepysaurus. Then . . .

Scraaak went the Sleepysaurus, this way, and *craaak* went the Sleepysaurus, that way. *Scraaak! Craaak! Scraaak! Craaak!* The Sleepysaurus was moving. Lots of flowers and rock plants and little chairs the Old Ladies had put on the Sleepysaurus's back fell off.

It was heading for the gate.

"STOP!" we all cried. We were too late.

The Sleepysaurus left a great big hole where the gate had been.

"COME BACK!" we all shouted as we charged after it. There was a trail of potted plants and broken flowers and Old Ladies' chairs right down the middle of the road, as far as the ice-cream van. The ice-cream man wasn't there. He was in his house counting ice-cream money.

SCRUNCH! and then SLURP, GURGLE went the Sleepysaurus.

It ate all the ice-cream tubs and the lollies and the orange drinks and the wafers and the chocolate sticks and the ice-cream man's freezer, and then it ate the van.

"Any more where that came from?" asked the Sleepysaurus politely.

"No!" we said. "And you'd better go home quickly before the ice-cream man gets you!"

But the Sleepysaurus didn't go home. It went to the garage, and tried the petrol

*It ate all the ice-cream tubs and the lollies
and the orange drinks and the wafers and*

the chocolate sticks and the ice-cream man's freezer, and then it ate the van.

pumps, but it didn't like the petrol. It drank a bit of the canal, but the people on the boats started shouting when the water went down.

"So sorry," said the Sleepysaurus, and it *scraaak*ed and *craaak*ed away across the park, with us running after it.

The people on the canal boats were very cross about their water. They rang the police station, but they couldn't get through because all the lines were engaged. The ice-cream man was ringing about his ice-cream van and the garage man was ringing about his petrol pumps, and one of the Old Ladies was ringing about someone stealing the rock garden from our flats because she'd noticed it was gone.

The Sleepysaurus lumbered on. It drank the drinking fountain and the tiddler pool and the duck pond. It didn't drink much of the duck pond because all the ducks quacked at it, and the Sleepysaurus got scared. It had never seen a duck before. There can't have been ducks when there were Sleepysauruses. We caught up with it again at the swimming pool. We knew it was there because of the big hole in the dressing rooms, and the claw prints as big as prams round the deep end.

And the island. The island wasn't an island, but we told the policeman and the bargeman and the ice-cream man and the petrol-pump man that it was, when they came chasing after us.

"It's an island!" we said. "Now our swimming pool is a tropicana!"

The man from the swimming pool thought that that was a very good idea, although he didn't know where the island had come from. He got palm trees and he

"It's an island!" we said.

"Now our swimming pool is a tropicana!"

put them on the Sleepysaurus, and he set up a coconut stall.

The next day lots and lots of people came to swim there and three of the mums got jobs dressing up in grass skirts and dancing to Hawaiian music. We just watched and waited.

The day after that was very hot, and so was the next one and the next one. The heat made everybody cross, especially the Old Ladies. They went to the Mean Man's house and marched up and down outside it in their sun-hats. They all chanted:

"WE WANT OUR ROCK GARDEN BACK!" and "YOU STOLE OUR ROCK GARDEN!"

"No I didn't!" said the Mean Man.

"Yes you did!" cried the Old Ladies, and they chased him round and round his house until he hid up a tree. The Old Ladies chopped the tree down. The Mean Man fell through the roof of his greenhouse. His greenhouse was very, very hot.

"Let me out!" he cried.

"No way!" said all the Old Ladies, and they kept him in the greenhouse all day.

"I'm a bit sorry for the Mean Man," I said.

"Only a little bit," said Rashid.

"A little, little bit," said Niki.

We were sorry because it wasn't the Mean Man's fault, but we couldn't tell the Old Ladies about it because they wouldn't have believed us.

"It would be all right if the Sleepysaurus came back," I said.

That night we all went down to the swimming pool to speak to the Sleepysaurus about it. The pool was closed when we got there, but we got through the hole. The

Sleepysaurus was splashing about in the moonlight, like a baby in a bath.

"We've brought you some soap," we told the Sleepysaurus.

"Thank you very much," said the Sleepysaurus and *slurp-gurgle*, it ate the soap. It didn't like the soap much.

"Not very nice," it said, and lots of soapy bubbles came out of its mouth.

"You're supposed to wash with it!" we said.

"Sleepysauruses don't wash," said the Sleepysaurus. "They just take a little bath now and then, when it is hot."

"Very sensible," I said.

"I am very sensible," said the Sleepysaurus.

Then I had an idea.

"Well, now you've had your bath it is bedtime!" I said.

"Bedtime?" said the Sleepysaurus.

"Yes," I said. "Flowerbed-time!"

And I told it all about the Old Ladies running up and down our road picking up the flowerpots and the plants and chairs that had fallen off it.

"They're all very cross, because they've got no rock garden," I said. "That's why it is flowerbed-time!"

"I think you're right!" said the Sleepysaurus. "I'm getting sleepy anyway!"

And it got out of the swimming pool and *scraaak-craaak*ed all the way across the park and over the canal and up to the flats.

We thought the Old Ladies might spot it, because they were having an All Night Bring Back Our Stolen Rock Garden Vigil round the Mean Man in his greenhouse, but they'd all gone to sleep in their little tents. They came back to our flats in the morning,

*"Hip-hooray!" cried all the Old Ladies.
"Our rock garden is back!"*

and they saw our Sleepysaurus.

"Hip-hooray!" cried all the Old Ladies, throwing their hats and tent poles and tents and camping cookers and banners in the air. "Our rock garden is back!"

They settled down in the shade of the palm trees. Our mums and dads were very happy because they were fed up with listening to the Old Ladies marching about and singing protest songs. The Mean Man was happy because he was let out of his greenhouse. Even the Sleepysaurus was happy, because it didn't like baths much, except when it was very hot.

"That's all right for now," Rashid said. "But what will we do tomorrow? The Sleepysaurus might get hot again!"

"Don't worry!" I said. "Tomorrow it will *rain*!"

And it did.

*The Mean Man was angry and
splashed about in our yard.*

SLEEPYSAURUS
CATCHES COLD

Next day it rained. I *knew* it would. It didn't just rain. It poured and belted and it caught the Mean Man when he was moving the bins. We all cheered, and the Mean Man was angry and splashed about in our yard. We stayed inside and drew pictures of the Mean Man getting wet. All the Old Ladies stayed inside too, except Mrs Armitage. She likes the rain. She went out and sat in it.

"She's a walrus!" Rashid said.

"A whale!" Niki said.

"A mermaid!" I said. "A mermaid sitting on a rock!" That was because Mrs Armitage was sitting on the Sleepysaurus, underneath the palm tree. Then our grating got blocked, and the water started rising. It was great. We had a flood, like Noah. All the dads came out and sandbagged the doors. Our bins floated round the yard, and the Old Ladies rushed about in their Wellington boots rescuing their potted plants. Then the Old Ladies' hats blew off. They turned into hat-boats and floated round the yard, with the Old Ladies after them.

"Let's all make boats," Rashid said.

I used an old milk carton, with my hanky for a sail. Niki used a shoe box; it sank. But Rashid had the best boat. He got a tin bath from the shed. It was a *real* boat. We put on old clothes and sailed it in the yard. Rashid was captain. There was a storm and we sank, just off the coast of Africa. The Sleepysaurus was Africa, but we didn't tell it. I don't think Sleepysauruses *know* about

Africa. The Mean Man came and grabbed our boat.

"Clear off!" he told us.

Our mums got him. They scolded him about the blocked grating. Our mums were really mad. The Mean Man rang the council and the council sent the fire engine and it was really great. There was water sploshing everywhere, and the Chief Fireman told the Mean Man off. We watched it all through Rashid's window, when we were having our lassi, which is a sweet nutty yogurt drink Rashid's mum makes.

The water went down. We put our boots and raincoats on and helped the firemen with the hose. I rang the fire-engine bell. The firemen said we could come down to the station sometime and play snooker. Then the firemen went away.

All the Old Ladies started mopping up

and we built a fort with the sandbags and defended it against the Mad Moppers. We got wet again, but we had a good time. Then...   Sniff and

sniff and

sniff-sniff and

sniffle.

"Who's got the sniffles?" Rashid's mum asked, and she made us all go inside. But *we* hadn't got the sniffles. We weren't doing the sniff and the sniff and the sniff-sniff and the sniffling. It wasn't us. It was the Sleepy-saurus.

"You shouldn't have been out in the wet!" Rashid's mum said, and she sent us all home.

Sniff.

"Don't sniff, Marigold," said my mum and she gave me a big hanky.

Sniff.

Niki's mum gave her hot honey and lemon.

Sniff-sniff.

Rashid's mum gave him tea with ginger to stop the sniffles.

Then, SNIFFLE.

We were all sent to bed. It wasn't bad. We hadn't got colds, but we got tissues and sweeties and halvah and comics and fried cashews and mango and cheese-and-onion crisps and we got read stories.

But the sniff and the sniff and the sniff-sniff and the sniffling still went on.

"It isn't us!" we told our mums, but they wouldn't believe us, and we wouldn't tell them who *was* sniffling, because they don't know about our Sleepysaurus. He is our Sleepysaurus, not anybody else's, and we weren't going to give our secret away.

"Must be the Mean Man!" Rashid told his mum.

"Must be the Old Ladies!" I told mine.

And Niki told her mum it must be the dads who'd caught colds, moving the sandbags. But the Old Ladies were tucked up in bed with their potted plants and hot beef tea and all the dads had gone off to thank the firemen at The Coach and Horses.

"It *is* you," said the mums. "It must be,

because it isn't us!" Then...

AAAAAHHHHHTIIIIIISSSSSSSSSSSSSS-
SSSSSHHHHOOOOOOOOOOOOOOOOOO!

All the walls shook, and the ornaments
rattled. The Old Ladies leapt under their
beds, and spilled beef tea all over their potted
plants. The plants wilted. The TV aerials
blew wonky right in the middle of the
news. The Mean Man's bins blew about the
yard. Tiles flew off the roof. Rashid's mum

swallowed her false teeth. Niki's mum fell off her chair. My mum blessed herself, and blessed me, and rang our gran to see if she was all right, but all the telephone lines were down, so she couldn't get through. All the dads and the firemen came racing up from The Coach and Horses to find out where the explosion *was*, but the explosion *wasn't*.

"Wait and see if it happens again!" said the Mean Man, who had come running up the hill in his pyjamas to find out who'd blown up the flats.

It didn't happen again.

There was only an occasional sniff and a sniff and a sniff-sniff and one bigger than usual sniffle and no

AAAAAHHHHHTIIIIIISSSSSSSSSSS-
SSSSHHHHOOOOOOOOOOOOOOO!

although we waited for one.

We were very worried. We didn't want them all finding out about our Sleepy-saurus. I don't know how the Sleepysaurus stopped its sneezes. It must have held its breath and counted.

The dads and the firemen went back to The Coach and Horses and the Mean Man went back to his house in his pyjamas (after fixing all the bins again) and our mums put their feet up and all the Old Ladies wrung out their plants and got back into bed.

I wanted to have Marigold's Emergency Meeting to Keep Our Sleepysaurus Secret but I couldn't, because my mum wouldn't let me out in case of explosions.

We had my Emergency Meeting in the morning instead, Rashid and Niki and me. We held it on the Sleepysaurus.

The sniffling was still going on, but it was very small sorry-for-itself sniffles that

"I'm a Sickysaurus!" said the Sleepysaurus
and it gave a dry, miserable cough.

we heard, not big ones.

"Are you all right?" I asked the Sleepy-saurus.

"No," said the Sleepysaurus.

"What's the matter with you?" asked Rashid.

"I'm a Sickysaurus!" said the Sleepy-saurus and it gave a dry, miserable cough.

"Don't do that!" I said. "All the mums will come rushing."

"Don't care!" said the Sleepysaurus. "I'm sick!" It kept mumping and grumping but it didn't *scraaak* or *craaak* once.

"We'll get you better," we told it. But the trouble was that we didn't know how to get it better.

"Hot tissues and sweeties?" I said.

"Tea with ginger," Rashid suggested.

"Or hot honey and lemon," said Niki.

"We haven't got enough tissues or

sweeties or tea with ginger or hot honey and lemon," I said. "It would take tons and tons and tons to cure a Sleepysaurus."

"Get the doctor?" Rashid suggested.

"Or the vet!" said Niki.

"Or a mining engineer!" I said.

So I went to the Sleepysaurus and I asked it if it would like the doctor or the vet or a mining engineer.

"What do they taste like?" said the Sleepysaurus.

"Don't know," I said. "They're people."

"I don't eat people," said the Sleepysaurus, irritably. "But I might try a little cement."

We got it some cement, but it ate only one bucketful. It was a big bucket, but a very small snack for a Sleepysaurus.

"Did you go all purry inside?" Niki asked hopefully.

"No," said the Sleepysaurus. "I'm sick and I'm miserable and I couldn't eat another thing."

We were very worried. We went round asking everybody how to cure a cold, but nobody could tell us. They said all the things we knew already, like aspirins and tea with ginger and hot honey and lemon. I even asked the Mean Man.

"How do you cure a cold?" I asked.

"I'b dond dnow!" he yelled, and he sneezed all over me. "Amd id I dib dnow I'b cure byself burst!"

We thought catching a cold served the Mean Man right! We didn't ask the Old Ladies because they all had colds too, and were curled up round their soggy plants. Our mums were running round looking after them. They brought the Old Ladies warm blankets and good books from the library, and kept them cosy.

"Best thing for a cold!" my mum said. "Keeping cosy!" I thought about it. Then I went out and looked at the Sleepysaurus. It is a very BIG Sleepysaurus, and our yard isn't cosy.

"We've got to keep it cosy!" I told Rashid and Niki.

"How?" they said.

"Wrap it up warm, and get it good books," I said.

"It can't read," Rashid said.

"We could read to it," I said.

"Or let it watch television," Niki said.

"I don't think there's much on television that would interest a Sleepysaurus," I said, but I asked it about the reading.

"That would be very nice," said the Sleepysaurus. So we read to it. We read it lots of stories, but it only liked the ones with cement in them, and there aren't many of those.

It kept on *sniffling*.

"Are you cosy?" I asked it.

"I'm cold, not cosy!" it said.

We didn't know what to do, because all the Old Ladies had the warm blankets, and anyway the blankets weren't big enough.

Then I had my big idea.

It was the Big Knit Competition.

"What's that?" all the Old Ladies asked, because they were bored stiff sitting in bed reading good books and watching television and being looked after by our mums.

"It's a competition to see who can knit the biggest blanket!" I said.

"What does the winner get?" asked the Old Ladies. I thought a bit, and I thought a bit more and then I said, "The winner gets all the blankets!"

All the Old Ladies cheered, and then they got out their wool and started knitting.

Knit-knit-knit-knit-knit-knit-knit... We got *tons* of blankets. Then we held our Big Knit Exhibition on the Sleepysaurus. All the mums and dads came, and the neighbours and the Mean Man. He tried to sneak off with a blanket, but we wouldn't let him.

"Mine's best!" cried all the Old Ladies. "When do I get my prize?"

"Tomorrow," said Niki, cunningly.

"Or possibly the next day," said Rashid craftily.

"Just as soon as the exhibition closes!" I said, because I didn't want to say what day. I didn't want to say what day because I wasn't going to give them their blankets until the Sleepysaurus was better.

The Old Ladies went away grumbling about whose blanket was best.

"Happy now?" I asked the Sleepysaurus.

"I'm cosy," said the Sleepysaurus.

And it didn't sniff or sniff-sniff or sniffle all that day or the next day. But the next night it went . . .

Scraaak . . . Craaak . . . Then, *slurp, gurgle* . . . it ate up all the cement and bricks and coal and concrete and old tin we could bring it with some tar from the dump for afters.

"I'm better!" said the Sleepysaurus. And it went to sleep. Gently, quietly, in our yard, without disturbing the Old Ladies or our mums and dads or anybody else.

Like a Sleepysaurus should.

THE

END